The Secret at the Seashore

New edition! Revised and abridged

By Laura Lee Hope

Illustrations by Pepe Gonzalez

Publishers · GROSSET & DUNLAP · New York

Revised and abridged by Nancy S. Axelrad.

Contents

1 Underground City 1

2 Money Clue 10

3 Fishy News 19

4 The Wrong Man 28

5 Lagoon Thief 36

6 A Floating Trick 46

7 Freddie Disappears 57

8 Chasing the Culprit 65

9 Island Hideout 74

10 Motorboat Mischief 85

11 A Lot of Loot 97

∎ 1 ∎

Underground City

"Look!" Flossie Bobbsey cried. She pointed to a group of police officers standing just beyond the entrance gate of Lakeside Amusement Park.

"Wowee! Police officers!" her twin, Freddie, exclaimed. He and Flossie were six years old.

Their brother, Bert, and sister, Nan, who were twelve-year-old twins, glanced at each other in bewilderment. "I wonder what happened," Bert said.

"Maybe we should come back another time," their mother, Mary Bobbsey, replied.

"Oh, Mom," Nan pleaded, "it must be all right, or they wouldn't have let us in."

Her mother smiled. She knew the twins loved a mystery, and they weren't happy until they solved it.

"Come on, everybody, let's investigate," Bert said eagerly.

His eleven-year-old cousin, Dorothy Minturn,

who was slender and had dark hair like Bert and Nan, darted after the other children. Ever since her cousins had arrived in Ocean Cliff, Dorothy had been looking for a mystery to solve.

The Bobbsey family had been visiting with Mr. Bobbsey's brother, Daniel; his wife, Sarah; and their son, Harry, who was the same age as the older twins. Mary Bobbsey had received a phone call from her sister, Emily Minturn, inviting the whole family to Ocean Cliff. Mrs. Bobbsey and the twins accepted gleefully. But the twins' father had to return home to Lakeport for a few days to take care of his lumber business. The Bobbseys' housekeeper, Dinah Johnson, who had been with the family, returned with him, because she was about to leave on a vacation of her own.

The first few days in Ocean Cliff had passed uneventfully. Suddenly there was a hint of excitement.

"Excuse me, officer," Bert said, approaching a policeman under a lime-colored awning. "Do you know what happened?"

The policeman's silvery badge sparkled as he explained that a man suspected of stealing a large sum of money had been traced to Lakeside Amusement Park.

"It's going to be tough tracking him down.

There are just too many places in this park to hide!"

"Who is he?" Nan asked. "And where was the money stolen from?"

"His name is Albert Garry, and he worked for Allied Cargo Airlines down the road. A big shipment of currency from Switzerland arrived early this morning, and as it was being unloaded, a lot of it disappeared."

"I hope *we* can find that man who stole the money," Flossie said earnestly. "What does he look like?"

"Well," said the officer, "Albert Garry is short and slim and has blond hair that sticks up at the top. If you do see anyone who fits that description, let me know. My name is Weaver."

As the children walked away, Freddie suggested, "Maybe he's hiding on one of the rides."

Bert overheard him. "That's a thought," he said. "While we're having fun on the rides, we can be on the lookout. Why don't we split up?"

Nan's eyes traveled to a roller coaster ahead.

"Dot," she said to her cousin, "you, Flossie, and I can go on that."

"Bert, will you go in the Underground City with me?" Freddie asked, pointing to a nearby ticket booth.

"It's fun," Dorothy put in. "You get in little boats that run on a cable through an underground canal. Along the sides are scenes of a make-believe city."

"What can Mommy and Aunt Emily do?" Flossie asked.

Mrs. Bobbsey nodded at a line of benches. "We'll sit and keep our eyes peeled for the culprit."

As she spoke, a clown with fuzzy red hair appeared from behind a refreshment stand and held out a basket of cotton candy in front of the children.

"Yummy!" Flossie exclaimed. She was ready to take one of the cones, but stopped as the clown leaned forward to talk.

"I saw you talking to that nice policeman," he said in a kindly voice.

"We're going to help him solve a mystery," Flossie revealed. "We're detectives."

"Oh, you are? Well, then, maybe you can help me, too. I have a big secret."

"You do?" Flossie asked.

"I can't talk about it here. Come to the yellow tent later and bring your friends," he replied. "Don't tell anyone else."

"I won't."

He smiled, then turned away and left.

"What was that all about?" Nan asked her sister as she bought tickets for the roller coaster.

Flossie repeated what the clown had told her.

"Where's the yellow tent?" Nan asked Dorothy.

"Behind the lake. I can't imagine why he wants us to go there. I mean, it's just a big empty tent where they hold meetings sometimes."

When the three girls were finally seated in one of the little cars, a stout woman and a small man in a fishing hat sat down behind them.

"I'm going to put on my hat," Nan announced, setting it firmly on her head. As she did so, the car gave a jerk and started up the long incline.

Flossie clung to the metal bar in front of her.

"Hang on!" Dorothy cried as the car edged closer to the top, then hurtled down the steep grade.

"Whee!" Flossie squealed.

"Look at the lake!" Dorothy shouted over the roar of the car. It was about to spiral across the water.

The stout woman clutched the back of the girls' seat. "Aaaalbert!" she screamed.

Albert! Was it possible that the thief, Albert Garry, was sitting behind them? The girls did not dare turn around as the car raced along the track.

"Now, sweetie," the man said soothingly. But then the car jerked around a curve. "My hat!" he yelled, watching it sail into the air.

"Oh, no!" Nan gasped. The wind had caught her straw hat as well and snatched it from her head. Down, down the hat drifted toward the ground.

Soon the car reached the end of the ride and slowed to a stop. At once the girls turned to look at the man behind them. He was completely bald!

Dorothy leaned toward Flossie. "I didn't think he was the thief Albert," she said softly.

"I didn't think so either," Nan agreed. "He couldn't really hide on the roller coaster. Oh, well. Maybe I can find my hat, anyway."

The trio walked slowly around the base of the roller coaster, peering at the ground. When they reached the ticket booth again, Nan looked up.

"There it is!" she exclaimed. "On the merry-go-round!"

The merry-go-round wasn't turning. Sitting on the head of the tallest giraffe was Nan's hat!

Flossie giggled. "He looks funny!"

"Want to take a ride?" Dorothy asked, causing her young cousin's eyes to light up.

When the merry-go-round started again, Dorothy was astride the giraffe. She grabbed the hat and stretched forward to hand it to Nan, who was seated on a tiger in front of her.

Bert and Freddie, in the meantime, had climbed into a little two-passenger boat for the trip through the Underground City. Bert sat in the front seat, with Freddie directly behind him.

"Keep your hands inside the boat!" the attendant called as the boat began to move away.

The first few minutes of the ride were spent in total darkness. Then a scene appeared. It was a miniature school building with children moving in and out of the front entrance. Next to them in the playground was a tiny seesaw with two little figures bobbing up and down. Two others behind them were tossing a ball into a basket fastened to a pole about a foot high.

The boat glided past several more scenes. One of them showed a block of toy buildings at the end of which was a hotel. It was on fire!

"Look at the fire engine!" Freddie cried.

The toy engine was standing in front of the building as miniature fire fighters held a long hose through which streams of water poured over it.

"The fire fighters are rescuing the people!" Freddie exclaimed. He pointed to the side of the

building, where a tiny ladder stretched high to the top windows as brave little fire fighters swarmed into them.

Suddenly Freddie grabbed on to Bert's arm. "Look!" he whispered. "There's someone behind that middle building!"

"I don't see anyone," Bert protested.

"It was a man. He had blond hair that stuck straight up."

"You must be mistaken, Freddie," Bert said patiently. "How could anyone get behind there?"

Freddie said nothing as the little boat glided past a beautiful park with tiny trees and ponds and into another dark, spooky tunnel. Finally the riders emerged into the sunlight.

Mrs. Bobbsey, Aunt Emily, and the three girls were waiting on the platform. "Where's Freddie?" Flossie called out.

Bert turned around. The back seat was empty!

■ 2 ■
Money Clue

"Bert!" Mrs. Bobbsey cried in alarm. "Where's Freddie?"

Her older son was too stunned to speak. At that moment an attendant came forward to hold the boat. "Did you lose something?" he asked, seeing the stricken expression on Bert's face.

"Yes. My little brother!"

"Your brother?" The man looked startled.

"He was in the boat with me. I don't know where he went."

Mrs. Bobbsey panicked. "Maybe he fell out!"

"Now, take it easy, ma'am," the attendant said, trying to remain calm. "Kids often play tricks in the Underground City. We'll find him."

Mrs. Bobbsey gulped back tears while the attendant pushed a button, reversing the direction of the cable that pulled the boats. He jumped into the two-seater with Bert, and they started back through the tunnel.

"What did your brother like most about the Underground City?" the guide asked.

"The fire engines," Bert responded quickly. "Maybe that's where he is!"

"No doubt."

As Bert had predicted, Freddie was sitting contentedly in front of the fire scene, watching the entrance to the tunnel.

"Hi, Bert!" he called. "I knew you'd come back to get me."

The cheerfulness in Freddie's voice only made his brother frown. "Hey, who said you could leave the boat without telling me?" he scolded.

"No one," Freddie replied, lowering his eyes.

The attendant grabbed a hook in the wall and stopped the cable.

"I was sure I saw Albert Garry behind those little buildings, but you wouldn't believe me. So I decided to jump out and look for myself."

"What did you find?" Bert inquired. He helped Freddie squeeze into the seat next to him for the ride back outside.

"Nothing," Freddie murmured, "but I know I saw him!"

When the boat reached daylight again, Mrs. Bobbsey and the others looked greatly relieved. "Freddie, don't you ever do such a thing again!" his mother scolded after she had thanked the attendant.

"I'm sorry, Mommy," the boy said meekly. "I didn't mean to scare you."

Dorothy felt sorry for her small cousin and wanted to cheer him up. "May we go to the Enchanted Castle, Mom?"

"Enchanted Castle? Where's that?" Freddie asked immediately.

"It's here in the park," Dorothy said, adding mysteriously, "I won't tell you any more than that, because it's a secret!"

"We'll go after lunch," Aunt Emily said.

"I want a million hot dogs and a bucket of ice cream!" Freddie announced.

"And I want two million hot dogs and two buckets of ice cream!" his twin sister added.

But when they had taken their places in a small restaurant, Freddie settled for two frankfurters and Flossie for one.

"What happened to the million hot dogs you were going to eat?" Bert teased his brother.

Freddie grinned. "I'd be too stuffed to have fun at the castle!"

As the visitors left the restaurant, they met Officer Weaver on the way in. He looked very hot and very tired.

"Did you find the thief?" Bert asked.

The policeman shook his head. "Not yet," he replied. "We've been over every inch of this park. Maybe Garry never came here at all."

"But I saw him!" Freddie exclaimed. "In the Underground City!"

The officer appeared doubtful.

"I did, really I did," Freddie said.

"A couple of our men went through that place from top to bottom," came the reply. "Frankly, I don't see how he could be there."

Freddie was about to say something more, but decided otherwise. Instead, he and the other children promised to remain on the lookout for Garry and started off toward the Enchanted Castle. In the distance, they could see a building that looked like a small castle. Bright-colored flags flew from the turrets as the sound of tinkling music spread through the warm air.

"This is 'citing!" Flossie exclaimed.

In front of the castle was a small grassy oval with a fancy white iron bench. "I've already been in it and know the secret, so I'll wait for you here with Mom and Aunt Mary," Dorothy said.

While she and the two women went to sit down, the four Bobbsey twins walked to the entrance. The outside door was closed. Fastened to the wooden frame was a gold sign. It read:

This is the house of the magic princess. She invites all children to enter. If you catch the princess, she will grant your wish.

Nan pushed open the door, causing a bell to tinkle gently. Beyond was a narrow corridor with a stairway at one side and a wide doorway on the other.

"Let's go in there," Bert said.

The four children entered the room, which was furnished with little gold tables and chairs. There, in front of the fireplace, stood a beautiful young princess!

She had long yellow curls and twinkling blue eyes. Her dress was made of a soft silvery material, like the little net bows on her shoulders, and in her hand was a silver wand with a glittering star on the top.

"She's bee-yoo-ti-ful!" Flossie sighed.

"I'll catch her!" Freddie called out, running toward the fireplace.

But the princess raised her wand and a curtain swept in front of her. Instantly Freddie pulled it aside. "She's gone!" he said.

"You scared her away!" Flossie cried, tears of disappointment tumbling down her face.

"I was only trying to catch her!" her brother retorted.

"Maybe she went up the chimney," Nan said.

Bert walked over and peered up into the opening. "I don't see her, and besides, there aren't any steps here."

"I guess magic princesses don't need steps,"

Flossie said sadly. "They just make themselves invisible."

"Let's look around the house," Nan suggested.

The children wandered through the first floor. Next to the room with the fireplace was a little dining room. The table was set with pink-and-white dishes, and there was a bouquet of tiny roses and forget-me-nots in the center.

"How cute! Maybe the princess is hiding under the table!" Flossie said, bending over to see. To her disappointment, no one was there.

Next the children explored the second floor. There they found two little bedrooms, completely furnished with frilly white curtains at the windows and pretty floral coverlets on the beds.

Again the twins looked everywhere, under the beds and in the closets, but still there was no sign of the golden-haired princess.

As they returned to the first floor, however, Flossie noticed a face at the window. It was painted white and had two circles for eyes and big cherry-red lips. "Mr. Clown!" she exclaimed, running forward.

"Don't forget to come to the yellow tent," he said. "And remember, it's a secret!"

"Who was that?" Freddie asked.

"Mr. Clown. He wants us to go to the yellow tent."

When the twins came out of the castle, Dorothy hurried to greet them. "Did you catch the magic princess?"

"No," they chorused sadly.

"Maybe you will next time," Dorothy said. "I had to go there twice before I did."

As they headed in the opposite direction, they noticed a booth filled with straw hats, beach bags, and colorful woven sandals. Seated on a stool next to them was a little girl about seven years old. Flossie darted toward her on impulse and said cheerfully, "Hi, my name's Flossie. What's yours?"

"Hi, I'm Cindy Weller," the wavy-haired girl said. "This is my mommy's booth."

As she spoke, her mother appeared from behind the booth.

"We're looking for a thief," Flossie announced.

"The same one the police are searching for?" Mrs. Weller asked.

Flossie nodded as the other children ran to join her. Bert explained that the police were beginning to think that Albert Garry hadn't come to the amusement park after all.

"I saw him," Cindy remarked.

"Are you sure?" Nan asked. "When?"

"Just this morning. He was running over there." She pointed to the Underground City.

"He was carrying a big paper shopping bag. It was white and had blue stars on it!"

"Maybe the money was in it!" Freddie exclaimed.

"It's a clue anyhow!" Bert said. "Have you told Officer Weaver?"

"Yes, but he says it could have been someone else," said Cindy.

"There he is now," Nan said.

She ran toward the policeman, who had stopped to get a drink at a water fountain, and talked with him about Cindy's story.

"Well, maybe it *was* Garry," Weaver admitted wearily. "I'll order another search."

The police officer spoke into the small transmitter he was carrying and went to the ticket booth of the Underground City. After a short conversation a man came out and hung a "Closed" sign on the window.

"We'll close the Underground City for a while," said Weaver. "We'll turn on all the lights inside. That way we won't miss anything."

"May I go with you?" Bert asked eagerly.

After a moment's thought, Officer Weaver agreed. "Okay, but stay behind me. I don't want you to get hurt."

Bert ran back to report to his mother as three more policemen joined Officer Weaver. "All right," she said. "But be careful. Aunt Emily and I will wait for you near Mrs. Weller's booth."

The Underground City looked very different to Bert with all the lights on. To his surprise, there were walkways behind the scenery.

"These are service walks for the attendants," Officer Weaver explained. "They can take care of the exhibits without having to step in the water."

The searchers walked through the underground tunnel together, scanning both sides closely for the thief. But he was nowhere to be seen.

Freddie and the girls, meanwhile, were walking around the park.

"Maybe we can find another clue to the mystery," the boy had said.

However, like the searchers in the tunnel, they saw nothing unusual. The rides were busy, and the grounds were full of strollers. Then suddenly Nan stopped short. Not far away on a small bench was a big white shopping bag with blue stars on it. It looked just like the one Cindy had described!

Was the stolen money inside it?

▪ 3 ▪
Fishy News

Excited, Dorothy ran to look inside the bag. But just as she was about to pick it up, the stout woman whom the girls had seen on the roller coaster waddled back from the drinking fountain.

"Would you like a piece of taffy, dear?" she asked Dorothy. She opened the shopping bag and pulled out a large candy box.

Dorothy blushed in confusion. "N-no, thank you," she stammered, and hurried back to the other children.

Flossie and Freddie were too overcome with giggles to say anything. Nan smiled sympathetically. "I guess we'd better go find Mom," she said.

"We can't," Flossie blurted out. "I mean, not yet. We have to go to the yellow tent."

Nan bit her lips. "Is it far from here?" she asked her cousin.

"Not really," Dorothy said. "It's over there." She pointed toward a row of booths that led to an information building. "Follow me."

In a little while the visitors were standing on the other side of the building. There was nothing to see, however, except a rolling green hillside checkered with pathways.

"Where's the yellow tent?" Flossie asked.

"I thought it was there," Dorothy said, motioning at a clump of trees. "Guess we'll have to ask somebody."

She turned on her heel and headed into the information building. When she returned, she said, "The tent's at the bottom of the hill. Do you still want to go?"

"We have to. Mr. Clown is waiting for us," Flossie said.

"So is Mom," her sister reminded her somewhat anxiously.

"Pleeeeez," Flossie begged. "I promised."

"I still think we should make sure it's okay with Mom."

"I'll go check," said Dorothy. "I know my way around here better."

"Okay," Nan said. "We'll wait here."

But Flossie was getting impatient, and she ran off in the direction of the tent.

"Flossie!" Nan called. "Come back!" But her little sister wouldn't stop.

"Come on, Freddie," Nan said. "We'd better go after her."

They followed a twisting path that led past a rose garden surrounded by boxwood hedges.

"There she is!" Nan said. "And there's the yellow tent!"

It stood beyond the footbridge of a small turquoise pond that was surrounded by lanterns.

When Nan and Freddie caught up with Flossie, she was peeking inside the tent. "I don't see Mr. Clown," she said. "Where is he?"

Ignoring her sister's question, Nan scolded Flossie for having run off. "Dot will wonder where we are. Let's hurry back immediately!"

But the little girl noticed something red and fuzzy poking out from behind a tree.

"Mr. Clown!" she cried gleefully, expecting an answer in return. When none came, everyone went to investigate.

"Mr. Clown?" Freddie called, dashing behind the tree.

"There he is," Nan said, giggling.

"Where?"

She picked a wig off the tree trunk and twirled it on her finger. "Here."

Flossie frowned in puzzlement.

"Why would Mr. Clown leave his wig in a tree?" Freddie asked.

Nan shrugged. She led the others back to the

tent. "Maybe there's another clue inside." Nan saw a shred of paper lying next to the entrance. Before she could pick it up, a loud cracking noise interrupted from outside.

"Uh-oh!" Freddie exclaimed, running out of the tent with the others. To their horror, part of the bridge had collapsed!

Nan glanced at the pond that separated the children from the rest of the park. Waves rippled in the distance. What had happened? Had someone come to the tent site and tampered with the bridge? Looking at the wig, she wondered if Mr. Clown had left it in the tree to lure the children across the bridge.

"Now what'll we do?" Flossie asked.

Nan gave her a cross look, but she didn't scold her sister again because she seemed frightened.

"The water can't be too deep," Nan said. "Maybe we can wade across."

As she spoke, Freddie rolled up his jeans, took off his shoes, picked them up, and stepped into the pond. Flossie and Nan did the same, and in a little while they were safely ashore.

When they returned to Mrs. Weller's booth, they found Bert, Dorothy, their mother, and Aunt Emily all talking to Cindy and her mother.

"What happened to you?" said Dorothy. "When I got back to the information booth, you were gone."

Nan explained what had happened.

"Next time, you listen to Nan, Flossie," Mrs. Bobbsey said seriously. "It's a good thing you all got back safely."

Bert suddenly caught sight of the fuzzy red wig in Nan's hand. "What are you planning to do with that?" he asked.

"Return it, I guess."

"Why don't you leave it here? Cindy and I will be glad to take it over to Lost and Found," Mrs. Weller said, prompting Nan to set it on the counter. "And we'll tell the groundskeeper about the bridge, too."

"Thanks, Mrs. Weller," Nan said.

"Did the police find Albert Garry?" Freddie asked his brother.

Bert shook his head glumly.

"Well, we've all had a very exciting day anyway," Aunt Emily remarked. "It's late, and your uncle will be wondering where we are."

"Not only that," Mrs. Bobbsey said, "but also your father is due in this evening."

"I hope you'll come back again," Cindy said.

"Oh, we'd like to," Flossie replied. "We want to catch the magic princess!"

But as the older children left the park, they were thinking about other things. Where was Albert Garry? And what or who had caused the footbridge to collapse?

*   *   *

The next morning Bert telephoned Officer Weaver at police headquarters.

"I guess Garry wasn't at Lakeside after all," the officer told him. "The police in a town fifty miles up the coast are holding a suspect. They're sure he's the one we want."

Bert gulped. "Oh. Well . . . I'm glad he was caught."

"A couple of our men and one of the officials from the airline have gone up there to identify him," Weaver went on. "Looks like the case is closed."

When Bert told the other children the news, Nan said, "They really solved that mystery fast, didn't they? Let's tell Dad."

Mr. Bobbsey had arrived in Ocean Cliff on schedule and had already heard details of the twins' adventure in the park.

"But I wanted to help capture Garry," Freddie moaned.

"Look at it this way," Dorothy said. "At least we'll have more time to play on the beach."

Hearing the remark, her father came into the room. "How would you twins like to learn a little surf-casting?" he asked. "Your dad and I are going down to the beach to do some fishing."

Everyone was eager to go and hurried to put on swimsuits. When they arrived on the beach,

Uncle William was already there. The children watched as he deftly swung his pole around and sent the line whizzing out into deep water.

"Wow!" Bert exclaimed admiringly.

"It looks easy," Dorothy said, "but really it's awfully hard."

"Come here, everybody," Uncle William called. "I'll give you a lesson."

He showed Bert how to hold the pole. Then he stood behind his nephew, guiding his arms around, and finally telling him when to cast. The line spun through the air but fell short of Uncle William's mark.

"Not bad," Mr. Minturn said encouragingly. "Try again."

Bert grasped the long pole firmly with both hands and swung it back. This time the line shot out farther. He pulled it in and tried once more.

"I've got something!" Bert cried.

"Reel it in! Let's see what it is!" his uncle said.

Steadily Bert wound in the reel. Something dark broke the water.

"It's a black fish!" Flossie squealed.

Nan ran down to the water's edge to get a better look. "No, it isn't," she replied, laughing. "It's a piece of driftwood!"

Bert grinned and handed the pole back to Freddie. "Your turn," he said with a sigh.

Uncle William repeated the demonstration. "Ready?" he said to his younger nephew.

With a look of determination, Freddie swung it back and then snapped the pole forward.

"Oh, Uncle William!" Freddie exclaimed. "I have a bite!"

At the same moment, Flossie let out a small shriek. "My hair! It's caught!"

Nan and Dorothy ran immediately to her side. The fishhook was snagged in Flossie's blond curls!

While the two girls helped untangle them, Freddie laughed. "I caught a curly fish," he said.

"I'm no fish," Flossie answered indignantly.

"You sure aren't," her uncle said. "Well, Freddie, my boy, I guess we'd better clear the area next time." He turned to see Mr. Bobbsey who was coming across the sand with a newspaper in his hand.

"Daddy! Daddy!" Flossie called, scurrying toward him. "Uncle William is teaching us how to fish!"

"Oh, he is, is he? That's great!" her father said. He opened the paper as the other children gathered around him. "Maybe you can catch this whopper without too much trouble, then!"

■ 4 ■
The Wrong Man

Bert and Nan read the news story. "They haven't caught the airline thief yet!" Bert said.

"No?" Dorothy asked.

"The man who was arrested yesterday wasn't Albert Garry!" Bert continued, his pulse racing. "I'm going to find out what happened."

Leaving the two men behind, the children all ran into the house. In a few minutes, Bert had Officer Weaver on the phone.

"The man they caught only looked like Garry," the officer said. "He's probably still hiding in this area. We've got patrols on every road."

"Officer Weaver," Bert said, "was the stolen money marked in any way? Can it be identified?"

"No, but I understand that most of it was in large denominations."

When Bert revealed this to the other children, Freddie clapped his hands in excitement. "Let's go look for the money," he said, dashing to the front door.

"Whoa!" Aunt Emily called after him. "How about holding off for just a little while longer? I have a surprise for you."

"You do?" Freddie asked gleefully.

"I do. But it's at the train station."

"Mom always has nice surprises," Dorothy confided to Nan. "But what could it be?"

When they reached the station lot, the children watched eagerly as the train came to a halt and the passengers began to get off.

Suddenly Bert cried, "It's Hal!" That was the twins' nickname for their cousin Harry.

Harry Bobbsey grinned and waved as he swung down from the train steps. All the twins greeted him warmly.

"Your aunt Emily called Mom yesterday and invited me," Harry explained. "Was I happy! Things have been pretty quiet at the farm since you all left."

On the way to the house, the twins told Harry about their adventures at Lakeside as well as their attempts to capture the airline thief.

"It didn't take you long to find another mystery," Harry said. "Maybe I can help you solve this one, too."

It was decided that the older detectives would walk to the local shopping center and question the shopkeepers. "If anybody tried to change big money, I'm sure they'd remember it," Bert reasoned.

The first place they went to was a drugstore. When the children posed the question, however, the man shook his head. "I haven't seen a bill like that in a long time," he said. "Sorry."

Despite visits to several other shops, the story was the same. "We're not very lucky today," Nan said in a discouraged tone.

"I'm beginning to think Garry hasn't tried to spend any of the money," Bert replied. "If we don't get a clue pretty soon, we'll have to give up."

"Now, you know what Freddie and Flossie would say to that." Nan smiled. "We don't want to give up!"

The next store they visited was a small grocery. The only man in sight was busy unloading cartons and putting cans of food on a shelf.

"Be with you in just a minute!" he called. He took an empty carton to the back and then returned. "What can I do for you?" he asked.

Bert mentioned the stolen money.

"You know," the man replied, "someone did come in with a big bill just a few minutes ago. I couldn't give him change, so he left."

"What did he look like?" Dorothy inquired.

"Well"—the grocer thought a moment—"he was kind of short and had light hair." The man glanced out the window. He pointed toward the street. "There he is now!"

"I don't see him," Nan said excitedly.

"That blond man going past the record shop," answered the grocer.

The children thanked him and ran from the store. In front of them stood four girls.

"Hi, Dot!"

"Hi!" Dorothy said, intending to keep running. But her friends blocked the way.

Quickly she introduced the Bobbseys. "I'm sorry," she said. "We have to go. We're in a hurry."

"Are you going to be in the Water Carnival contest on Sunday?" one of the girls shouted.

"I guess so—maybe." By now the other children had run down the street. "Did we lose Garry?" Dorothy asked, catching up to them.

"He went into that brick building at the end of the block," Nan said.

"That's the library," Dorothy told her.

"Maybe he's going to hide his loot in there," Harry said.

The children raced toward the building and hurried inside. "There he is!" Nan whispered.

A small blond man stood by the desk in the center of the room. As Bert strode boldly toward him, he looked up and smiled at the children.

"Hello, Dorothy," he said. "Are these your cousins, by any chance?"

"H-hello, Mr. Crampton," Dorothy replied. "I—we thought—" Her face crimson, she turned to the others. "This is Mr. Crampton. He's a friend of my dad's."

Harry and the twins acknowledged the introduction. Then, as quickly as possible, they dived for the door again. Once outside, they all burst out laughing.

"Can you imagine?" said Nan, giggling. "Chasing Uncle William's friend!"

"I'm so embarrassed!" Dorothy said.

"*You're* embarrassed? What about me?" Bert confessed. "I almost grabbed him before he turned around."

Harry chuckled. "Talk about false clues."

"I guess it's too late to do any more sleuthing today," Dorothy said.

Later, when the children told Freddie and Flossie about chasing Mr. Crampton, they laughed until their sides ached. They were still talking about it when the telephone rang.

"Dottie!" her mother called a minute later. "It's Keith Bingham."

Dorothy darted to the phone. "Hi, Keith!" she said, pausing to listen. "No, really?" She hung up and raced back to her cousins. "I guess everybody is going to be in the contest."

"What contest?" Flossie asked.

Dorothy explained that once a year Lakeside Amusement Park held a special contest for all the children in the area. "We decorate our boats and wear costumes, then parade through the park lagoon past the judges. There'll be lots of prizes," Dorothy concluded. "Keith wants us to ride with him! What do you think?"

"I think it's 'citing!" Flossie exclaimed.

The other children agreed. But the next morning while the girls were planning their special wardrobe for Sunday, Bert and Harry borrowed two bicycles from the Minturns.

They rode some distance along the beach before turning onto a long country road that led inland from the shoreline.

"See those woods over there?" Bert said after they had ridden a little while longer.

Harry looked toward the distant trees. "What about them?"

"Well, it's just a hunch, but I think that thief, Garry, could be hiding in there. How about taking a look?"

"Okay," Harry said enthusiastically. "Dot says Indians roamed through there long ago. Maybe we can find some arrowheads." He had a collection of Indian relics that he had dug up when his father's fields had been plowed.

The boys crossed the road, then hopped off

their bicycles and propped them against a tree. "It's amazing how cool it is in here," Harry commented as they stepped into the forest.

"You can say that again."

"It's amazing how cool it is in here," the other boy repeated.

"Very funny. Just keep your eyes peeled for a campsite."

Saying no more, the pair walked along slowly, peering right and then left. The road was out of sight now, and the noise of traffic had completely faded away.

Suddenly Bert's foot hit something. He bent down and picked up a small stone. "Hey, look at this!" he said. "Do you think it's an arrowhead?"

Harry took the stone and examined it. It was heart-shaped, with sharp edges and a point. "I'm sure it is," he said. "Maybe we can find some more."

They got down on their knees to search among the brown pine needles. "Here's another one!" Harry exclaimed. He held up an odd-shaped stone with tiny dents in it.

"It looks different from the first one we found," Bert remarked.

"I know," Harry replied, "but it's practically identical to the one I have at home, and Dad said it was Indian!"

The cousins were so interested in looking for

more Indian relics that they forgot that they had come into the woods to search for the thief. Finally, when they had collected a pocketful of arrowheads, Bert looked up.

"It's getting late! We'd better go while we can still find our way out."

He turned to his right and began to walk briskly. Harry followed for a few minutes, then stopped. "This doesn't look right to me. I think we're going in the wrong direction."

Once again, Bert looked up through the tall trees. "If only it wasn't so cloudy," he moaned, "we could tell by the sun."

"We're lost, aren't we?" Harry said. "Let's build a signal fire. Maybe someone will see it."

"Not in the woods!" Bert said.

"Ssh!" Harry held up his hand. "I hear someone coming! Maybe it's Garry!"

Branches crackled as a figure moved closer through the underbrush. Hearts pounding, the boys held their breath.

Bert looked at Harry, then at the long dark shadow passing between the trees. It drifted from one to the other like a black monster crushing everything in its path.

One thing was certain. The strange silent beast wasn't Albert Garry.

Harry's knees shook. "M-maybe it's a bear!" he stammered.

■ 5 ■
Lagoon Thief

"Maybe it *is* a bear," Bert said, watching the shadowy creature vanish into the darkness. But then suddenly, as if from nowhere, it broke through the bushes in front of the boys.

"It's a cow!" Harry cried with glee.

"Not again!" his cousin said. "When we went on that picnic last time, we found a cow."

Harry chuckled as he thought of the incident at Meadowbrook. "Bessie."

"Looks like she got lonesome and followed you to Ocean Cliff," Bert teased.

"Oh, sure," Harry said, going along with Bert. "She took the train."

The animal flicked her tail and pushed slowly through the underbrush. Bert and Harry followed. In a few minutes the cow had made her way to the edge of the woods.

When the threesome emerged, a woman ran toward them from a nearby farmhouse. "Oh, you've found Daisy!" she said. "My husband just went to look for her."

Bert grinned. "We didn't exactly find Daisy," he explained. "She found us!" He told how he and Harry had been lost in the forest.

"I always said Daisy was smart!" the woman said. "Why don't you come into the house for something to eat. You must be hungry!"

After the boys had finished two glasses of milk and eaten a plate of cookies between them, the farmer's wife told them how to get to the road near where their bikes were. They thanked her and left.

That evening the children had a great deal to talk about. The minute the girls heard what had happened to Bert and Harry, Dorothy crept up behind them and gave a low *moooo!*

"Okay, okay. So I was scared of a cow," Bert said, grumbling good-naturedly. "I didn't know it was a cow."

Flossie giggled and let out another *moo.*

"Come on, Floss," Nan said quickly. "Let's show Bert our costumes!"

The girls dashed to their room with Dorothy. In a little while they reappeared in long skirts and blouses with shawls.

Nan curtsied. "Begging your pardon, sir," she said to her brother, "we're on our way west."

"You look super!" Bert replied.

Dorothy explained that they had found the old-fashioned clothes in a costume trunk that belonged to her mother. "We can fix up our motorboat to look like a covered wagon," she added eagerly.

"Well, if you're going to be pioneers," Harry said, "we want to be pioneers, too."

When Keith arrived the next day, all the boys agreed.

"We can wear our jeans," Bert suggested, "and moccasins. I brought an old pair with me."

"And we can use my new canoe, the *Swan*!" Keith exclaimed.

"Fantastic!"

Freddie tugged gently on his brother's arm. "What about Snoop? He wants to be in the carnival, too."

The other children laughed. What could a cat do in a water carnival?

"Snoop can be a black panther!" Freddie said. "I'll sling him over my shoulder!"

As he dashed away to find his cat, Harry and Keith decided to go buy moccasins for themselves. Bert, on the other hand, went with the girls to help trim the little motorboat. They took some loops of wire from the barn and made a frame for the wagon roof, then draped it with old white beach towels.

Standing back to admire their handiwork, Bert said, "I'll bet this is the only covered wagon that ever had a motor!"

The next morning was bright and clear. After church and lunch, the children hurried into their costumes and went to Lakeside.

When they arrived at the lagoon, it was packed with boats. Keith and Dorothy tied up their craft, and the contestants all jumped out onto the little dock.

At the registration desk, Flossie sidled close to her older brother. "We didn't bring Snoop," she whispered. "Doesn't he have to register?"

Bert grinned. "He's sleeping in the bottom of the canoe. We'll have to register for him."

Flossie laughed as she watched Bert list Snoop's name after hers and Freddie's. Afterward they listened carefully to the rules and instructions and started back to the boats. It was then that Keith realized his canoe was missing.

Nan, Flossie, and Dorothy ran to where he and the other boys were standing.

"Who could have taken it?" Dorothy asked, staring at the empty dock space.

"They stole Snoop, too!" Freddie cried.

By now a crowd had gathered around the

children. A man pushed his way to the center.

"That aluminum canoe—was it yours?" he said to Keith, drawing a nod from the boy. "About ten minutes ago I saw a man jump into it and paddle away. It seemed odd, because I had seen children arrive in the same canoe."

"Did you see which way he went?" Bert inquired.

"He paddled down to the end of the lagoon, then turned north into the lake."

"Come on, Keith, let's follow him!" Bert said. "May we take your boat, Dot?"

"Sure!"

"Can I go, too?" Freddie asked.

"You'd better stay here," Bert said, jumping into the boat with Harry and Keith.

Starting the motor, he turned the bow toward the open water and headed sharply north.

"It's going to be hard finding him around here," Keith said. "There are so many coves. He could have pulled into any one of them."

"Even so, he's paddling. We have a motor," Bert reminded Keith. "We can catch up to him."

For a while the only sound the boys heard was the sputter of the motorboat. They scanned the shoreline in silence, searching for the missing canoe.

"He's gone," Harry said finally.

Several times, though, Keith thought he saw

the canoe in the underbrush that grew down to the water's edge. But when Bert brought the boat closer to shore, it usually turned out to be the trunk of a dead tree that had fallen among the bushes.

Then, all of a sudden, Bert pointed ahead to a little cove. "Isn't that a canoe?"

Keith shaded his eyes. "Yes!" he cried. "Turn around!"

Bert deftly swung the boat in a wide circle and aimed for the cove. The next moment he ran his craft up on shore next to the canoe. It was the *Swan!*"

"We're coming, Snoop," Harry said.

"I hope he's still in the canoe," said Keith.

He and Harry jumped into the water and waded forward. To their relief the cat was sound asleep where they had left him—in his basket at the bottom of the canoe. Bert reached down and tickled him under the chin.

"Wake up, Snoop," he said. "It's time to go back to the Water Carnival."

The cat stretched and sat up.

"Look!" Harry said. "There's something behind the basket!" He leaned over and picked up a white cloth cap.

"This could be the thief's cap," Keith said, joining them.

"Allied Cargo Airlines," Bert muttered, reading the faded printing on the visor. "That's the place Albert Garry worked for."

"So Garry stole your canoe, Keith," Harry said.

"He has probably been hiding in the amusement park since last week," Bert added. "And he figured the carnival was his chance to get away."

"Maybe we can still catch him!" Keith said. "I mean, how far could he have gone?"

Quickly the boys scanned the area for signs of the suspected thief.

"I see footprints!" Bert shouted, leading the way to shoe tracks in the sand.

"Let's follow them. They *could* belong to Garry!" Keith declared.

Harry was also eager to pursue the trail, but his cousin hesitated.

"If we don't get back to the park," Bert said, "the girls can't enter the contest. Let's tell the police about this and have them come out here."

"You're right," Keith said. "You take the *Firefly*. It's faster. Harry and I will paddle the canoe."

When they arrived at last, Bert was already talking to a policeman, who said, "To think that crook has been hiding out here all this time and none of us has been able to catch him!"

As he spoke, an announcement interrupted

over the loudspeaker, asking all entries to line up at the end of the lagoon.

"I have to go," Bert said. "Excuse me, please."

He dashed toward the other children, who were admiring the lineup. In the first boat was a large paper dragon. Lit from inside by a flashing red light, its giant head seemed to be spouting fire.

"Ooh! It's scary!" Flossie quivered.

In the next boat were two boys dressed as clowns. They were pretending to have a boxing match with huge gloves made of balloons.

"Oh, look!" Nan laughed. "There's Columbus! Isn't he great? He's crossing the ocean and looking for the New World!"

She pointed to a rowboat filled with boys dressed as sailors from Columbus's time. In the center, with his foot up on one of the seats and holding binoculars, was "Christopher Columbus" himself!

The parade moved slowly past the reviewing stand. But as the pioneers' canoe glided into view, Snoop began to squirm on Freddie's shoulder.

"Snoo-oop!" Freddie chided the cat. "You're supposed to be a black panther!" A wave of laughter swept over the crowd as the animal yawned.

When the parade was over, the boats lined up

along the side of the lagoon where the judges could examine them more closely. There was loud applause as the announcement came for first prize. It went to the paper dragon.

"Second prize for the boat entry showing most originality goes to Dorothy Minturn and Nan and Flossie Bobbsey." Again the audience clapped enthusiastically.

The judge held up his hand. "Please, ladies and gentlemen," he said as someone handed him a message.

A hush fell over the waiting crowd.

"Boys and girls," the judge said, beaming at the contestants, "something very unusual has just happened. I have an extra-special surprise for one of you!"

The drums rolled to thunderous applause as the children held their breath.

■ 6 ■
A Floating Trick

"We have decided to give an extra prize today," said the judge. "It goes to the entry that gave us the biggest laugh—Freddie Bobbsey and his black panther, Snoop!"

Freddie grinned as the band struck up another lively tune and the winning boats swung around to the judges' stand to receive their prizes. The designers of the fiery dragon won sets of flippers, face masks, and snorkels.

The girls' prize was an inflatable rubber raft with paddles. Keith held his canoe steady while Freddie leaned forward to collect his prize. It was a large toy sailboat with three masts and several sails.

Freddie's eyes shone with happiness. "Wow! Thank you!" he said to the judges.

That night, before going to sleep, the girls were talking about the carnival. Dorothy started to giggle. "Why don't we play a joke on Bert and

Hal tomorrow?" she said, revealing her idea.

"That's great! They'll think it's a clue to some mystery!" Nan laughed.

After breakfast the next morning, the two boys strolled out to the porch while the girls disappeared to gather what they needed for the trick. Then Nan and Flossie followed their cousin upstairs and changed into swimsuits.

"Harry and I pumped the raft up for you," Bert said when the girls returned. "We'll get our trunks on and meet you at the beach!"

When she got there, Dorothy opened the towel she was carrying, laid the contents next to a piece of driftwood, and covered them with sand.

By the time Bert and Harry appeared, the girls were already pulling the raft into the water. Bert gave the younger children a ride, and afterward, the others took turns paddling.

Finally they all flopped down on the sand. Dorothy took a seat near the driftwood. "I think I'll go in again and get some of this sand off," she said, winking at Nan.

She waded out until the waves splashed over her shoulders, then came back and sat down by Bert. He and Harry were busy discussing the events of the previous day.

"I think we ought to go back to the cove where we found Keith's canoe," Bert said. "We might—" He stopped, his attention caught by something bobbing in the water. Instantly he got up and ran into the ocean. A moment later he flashed a brown bottle in his hand.

"What's that?" Dorothy asked innocently.

"There's a message inside!" Bert exclaimed.

All the children jumped to their feet. Harry was particularly excited. "Another mystery!" he said as the other boy came forward.

"It has chewing gum around the cork!" Bert remarked.

"Open it, Bert!" his little brother cried.

"Yes, open it! Open it!" Flossie exclaimed, her blue eyes snapping with mischief.

Bert picked up a shell and began to chip off the gum. Finally it fell away entirely, revealing the cork, which stuck up slightly from the neck of the bottle. Using the sharp point of another shell, Bert managed to pry out the cork.

"Hurry!" Freddie urged.

Bert pushed his finger into the bottle and worked out a rolled-up piece of paper.

"What does it say?" Harry asked.

Bert appeared totally bewildered as he read the message:

> *Help! I'm drowning!*
> *Moby Dick, the Whale.*

At the sound of the girls' laughter, Bert

looked up. "Very funny!" he said, squinting angrily.

The girls were still laughing at the success of their trick when Keith came to Dorothy's house after lunch. "Did you know Bert found a bottle with a message inside?" Dorothy greeted him.

"A message?"

Bert grimaced sourly. "They think they're so clever," he said, filling Keith in.

Keith laughed. Then he said, "How about going over to the cove on the lake where we found my canoe yesterday? That guy Garry hasn't been caught yet."

Nan, Dorothy, and Harry accepted eagerly, while Bert pretended to sulk.

"Bert?" Nan asked him. "Are you really, really mad at us?"

"No. I guess not," he said, softening. "Let's go follow those footprints!"

Freddie and Flossie, however, decided to stay home and sail the new toy boat at the lakeshore.

"May I paddle, Keith?" Dorothy asked.

"Sure, get in the bow," he replied, walking back to the stern.

When the others were seated, Dorothy gave the *Swan* a gentle push and jumped in. Then, with strong, even strokes, she and Keith paddled the canoe up the lake. Within a few minutes they had passed the Water Carnival area.

"It was about the fourth or fifth cove above here, wasn't it?" Keith called to the two boys in the center.

"Yes," they replied as everyone peered at the passing inlets.

"There!" Bert cried. "I think it was this one."

Dorothy and Keith turned the canoe and headed for the shore. "I see where Garry beached!" Keith said.

When the canoe touched shore, Dorothy leapt out and held the craft while the others disembarked. Then they pulled the canoe up onto the narrow sandy beach.

"I hope no one's rubbed out the footprints," Harry said worriedly.

"Are these the same footprints you saw?" Dorothy asked. She pointed to deep impressions in the sand that led diagonally away from the water.

"Yes," Bert answered. He darted ahead, following the tracks as far as he could, until the sandy stretch ended. "There's a path here!"

A narrow lane ran from the beach through the low underbrush. The ground was marshy, and the path extremely muddy, making it easy to trace the footprints. The children followed them until they reached the highway that ran along to the ocean shore.

"Now where do we go?" Keith asked, pausing by the side of the road.

"He could have gone in either direction," Nan said. "Or a car might have picked him up."

"Maybe he crossed the road." Bert ran to the other side of the highway. "I don't see anything here," he said sadly.

"We may as well go back to the lake," Dorothy said after Bert joined them again.

The children walked back across the spread of land that separated the highway from the water.

"Maybe we'll find something along the lakeshore," Bert suggested.

Soon they were walking at the edge of the lake not far from where Keith's canoe had been beached. They surveyed the ground closely but found nothing unusual. Finally they turned back to the canoe.

However, as Harry stepped into the craft, a small piece of paper at the edge of the water caught his eye. He bent down and picked it up. Then he called to the others, "Look at this!"

Bert raced forward and took the paper. "It's a torn ticket to the Underground City," he said.

"The Underground City!" the others echoed.

"Yes," Bert replied. "Maybe Freddie really did see Garry in there."

"We should take this to the police," Nan said. "It's evidence."

The children piled into the canoe again. This time they did not stay along the shore but paddled in a straight line toward Ocean Cliff. When they beached, they went straight to police headquarters, where they found Officer Weaver at a desk.

"Well, well, how are all the young detectives today?" he asked cheerily. "Any more clues for us? We still haven't caught the airline thief."

Bert presented the ticket. "We found this on the lakeshore."

"Hmph, then Garry must have been in the park," the policeman said. "We've already searched every inch of it and we haven't found him. I doubt he'd go back, but I'll put a special plainclothes guard at the entrance to the Underground City just in case he tries to get in there."

At the same time, Mrs. Bobbsey had taken Freddie and Flossie to a little cove on the lakeshore. A breeze had filled the sails of the toy boat and sent it flying across the narrow strip of water that formed the inlet.

"It's really fast!" Freddie declared proudly. He ran along the shore and picked it up the moment it touched land.

Then Flossie launched the miniature craft.

After they had sent the boat across the cove several more times, she suggested they play Water Carnival.

"How can we do that when there aren't any other boats?" Freddie objected.

"We can dress this one up," Flossie insisted.

"But how?"

"With flowers and leaves," she said. "Things like that."

"Okay."

Freddie put the boat on the ground and helped his twin collect a few wildflowers and some trailing vines.

"Well, while you're doing that," their mother said, "I'll get some ice cream for all of us. Now, stay right here."

"We will," Flossie promised.

She and Freddie wound the vines around the masts and put the flowers on the deck, then set the small craft in the cool water again.

But the wind had changed. Instead of sailing across the cove, the boat headed out into the lake.

"Oh, stop it, Freddie!" Flossie shouted.

"I can't!" Freddie answered in distress. "It's too far out!"

The little boat was sailing farther and farther away from the shore. Freddie looked around in desperation. A short distance up the shore he saw a small rowboat tied to a dock and ran toward it.

"We'll have to use this," he said.

"Oh, Freddie, no," Flossie objected.

"Why not? I'll bring it back."

"But you don't know how to row!"

"I do so. It's not hard." He climbed in and took the middle seat. "Take that rope off the pole," he directed.

Flossie did as she was told. Then she climbed into the boat and sat down timidly. "Be careful," she said.

Freddie put his hands on the oars and began to row.

"You watch the sailboat," he ordered, "and tell me when we get close to it."

"It's going away!"

Freddie tried to row faster, but the oars were too heavy for him. As he yanked hard on one of them, it skimmed the water, splashing his sister from head to toe.

"Freddie!" she protested. "You can't row!"

Angrily he dug the oars into the water too deeply. They flew from his hands, and one struck him on the chest, causing him to tumble off the seat into the bottom of the rowboat. The oars unlocked and started to float away.

"Oh!" Flossie said, her lips trembling. "Are you hurt?"

Freddie struggled back onto the seat. "No. I'm okay." He tried to reach the oars, but they were too far away. "We'll have to paddle with our hands. You paddle on one side and I'll paddle on the other."

But this did not work either. The boat moved along quietly, blown by the brisk wind.

"Where's the sailboat?" Freddie asked.

"Way over there!" Flossie wailed. "We're never going to catch it!"

"Well, I'm not going home until we do!" her brother snapped back.

Both twins paddled very hard again, but the rowboat drifted out of their control. It headed around a bend.

"Look, Freddie!" Flossie cried out. "An island. Let's land there!"

"Yeah," Freddie agreed. "Maybe we can find someone to row us home and get my sailboat."

The wind blew the boat toward shore, causing it to bump as it came to a stop. "Come on, Flossie! Let's explore!" her brother exclaimed.

But as she rose from her seat, a harsh voice called out, "Leave here immediately! Don't land on this island!"

7

Freddie Disappears

"Who's that?" Flossie whispered, her face pale.

"I don't know, but I'm going to find out!" her twin said, stepping out of the boat.

"Come back, Freddie!" Flossie called, to no avail. She ran after him a short distance and called again, but Freddie paid no attention.

He disappeared along a dirt path, listening to the wind in the trees and waiting for the mysterious phantom voice to speak again.

"I wonder where it came from," he thought. Then his gaze fell on a piece of shiny white material hanging over a brier twig.

"Either somebody walked through here real fast and didn't watch where he was going," he thought, "or—" He picked up the material and looked at it more closely. Around the edge was a tiny patch of blue. Mr. Clown's costume flashed into his mind. It was satiny and white with big colored circles—yellow, green, and blue!

"Wait till Flossie sees this!" he thought, stuffing it in his pocket.

He darted back along the trail, unaware that someone was watching. In a moment, a giant canvas floated over his head, and Freddie tumbled to the ground.

"Help!" he cried. He kicked his arms and legs as the canvas was tied quickly around him, then dumped behind a tree.

Flossie, in the meantime, had gone back to the rowboat to wait for her brother. She looked at the darkening sky and felt a shiver. She stared at the path down which Freddie had walked, and she stepped back onto the sand.

"Freddie?" she called out timidly.

There was no answer. She walked on, peering through the trees for some sign of the boy, then took another step.

"Where are you, Freddie?" she said, letting the darkness swallow her up.

A few yards farther, she heard her brother's small, muffled voice and ran forward. "It's Flossie!" she cried, stopping to listen again.

Freddie's voice was louder but still muffled. Had he fallen into a hole? she wondered.

Then she saw the lump of canvas lying next to a tree and screamed. Hearing the cry, Freddie punched and kicked as hard as he could until he rolled into his sister's path.

"Get me out of here!" he cried.

"I'm coming! I'm coming!" she said. But the rope at the top of the opening was tied so tightly Flossie could not loosen it.

Freddie himself had tried sticking his fingers through the small hole but couldn't.

Now Flossie ran down the trail again. "Help!" she shouted at the top of her lungs.

At the same time, Nan and her companions had returned to the Minturns' and learned that Freddie and Flossie had disappeared. Now the older children were standing on the shore with Mrs. Bobbsey and Aunt Emily. Keith had brought up his canoe.

"Freddie! Flossie!" Nan and Bert yelled anxiously.

"Listen!" Dorothy commanded. "Someone's calling."

The five children became quiet. From far down the lake they heard the cry for help.

"That sounds like Flossie!" Nan said fearfully. "They must be in trouble!"

"We'll take my canoe and go after them!" Keith replied.

He and Bert jumped into the canoe and paddled swiftly out into the lake. Shortly the watchers on the bank saw two boats round the bend. The two boys were paddling the *Swan,* with Freddie and Flossie seated in it. The borrowed rowboat was tied behind, and inside was the canvas that had been used to capture Freddie.

"Thank goodness!" said Mrs. Bobbsey.

On the way back, Keith picked up the lost oars, and Bert rescued the sailboat.

"I got scared by that awful voice," Flossie remarked.

"What voice?" Bert asked quickly.

The small twins told him. Then Freddie explained how he had gone to investigate and found the shiny white material. He pulled it out of his pocket.

"I think it belongs to Mr. Clown," he declared, showing it to Bert.

"Maybe there's a connection between him and Albert Garry," the older boy said.

After they all reached the shore, Bert took Keith and Harry aside. "I'd like to know who was on that island," he said. "How about going over there?"

"I'm ready!" Harry said.

"So am I!" Keith added.

"No, you don't!" Mrs. Bobbsey interrupted. "Not today. I nearly lost two children over there. I don't want to worry anymore."

"Oh, Mom, we'll be careful," Bert pleaded.

"No, I said."

As Bert and his cousin walked back toward the group, Uncle William came hurrying from the Minturn boathouse. "Did any of you take the *Firefly* out?" he asked.

"No, sir," Bert replied. "We went in Keith's canoe. Has something happened?"

"I thought the motor was sputtering yesterday," Uncle William explained. "I planned to work on it before supper, but the boat's gone!"

"Gone!" Bert echoed in dismay. "We put it away last night. So it must have been taken this morning!"

As soon as they reached home, he phoned the police and reported the loss, along with Freddie's mishap.

"Do you suppose Albert Garry stole our boat?" Dorothy wondered as she and the other girls went to bed that night.

"I don't know, maybe," Nan said sleepily.

The girls had been asleep only a short while when they were awakened by a loud buzzing.

"What's that?" Nan cried, sitting up in bed.

Flossie and Dorothy also sat up. "It's my alarm clock!" Dorothy sighed, rubbing her eyes. "Sorry."

She turned on the light and stared at the clock

on the table next to the bed. "It's only eleven," she said, yawning and pressing the alarm switch. But, to her surprise, it was already in the off position.

"The noise seems to be coming from the bookcase," Nan observed. She and Flossie ran to look, and finally pulled an old battered clock from behind the books on the lowest shelf.

"Here it is!" Flossie exclaimed, and Nan shut off the alarm.

"That's funny," Dorothy said. "I don't remember putting a clock there." Puzzled, she climbed into bed again and turned out the light.

Half an hour later the room was filled with the sound of ringing once more.

"Not again!" Dorothy cried.

Flossie slept on, but Nan jumped out of bed. She ran over to the bookshelves and picked up the alarm clock. "This one's still off," she said.

The two girls scurried around the room, looking everywhere—under the beds, inside bureau drawers, any place they could think of. Then Dorothy opened the closet door. "It must be in here!" she called.

She pushed the dresses aside and picked a clock off the floor. "You know what?" Dorothy said to Nan. "I'll bet Bert and Harry did this to get even with us for tricking them with that bottle in the water."

The next morning they told Flossie about the second alarm clock going off, then went down to breakfast.

"Sleep well?" Bert asked as the girls took their seats at the table.

"Just fine!" Nan replied.

"We did hear some bells ringing, though," Dorothy said casually. "Did they bother you?"

"Didn't hear a thing," Bert said, smiling into his bowl of cereal.

A few minutes later Aunt Emily mentioned that Mrs. Weller had called to invite the children to visit with Cindy at the amusement park.

"I asked Mom again about going to the island," Bert whispered to Harry.

"What did she say?" the other boy asked, his eyes lighting up.

"'Maybe later.' In the meantime, we'll have to be satisfied going to the park. Anyway, I suppose we could find more clues there."

When the children arrived at the Lakeside Amusement Park, Cindy Weller was waiting for them at the gate.

"I want to catch the magic princess!" Flossie said.

"I've already done that," Cindy replied. "But you go ahead. It's lots of fun."

"Okay, we'll go to the castle," Bert agreed. "Harry hasn't seen it yet."

Nan and Dorothy, however, offered to help out at the booth. They had just finished rearranging the counter when a scrawny boy about ten came toward them.

"May we help you?" Nan asked.

"I want a cap with a visor," he said quickly.

Hearing him, Mrs. Weller called from the back of the booth, "There are some right behind you, girls."

Dorothy picked up the pile of caps and brought them to the counter. "Here you are," she said, selecting a small one. "Try it on."

"It's not for me," the boy said. "It's for some man."

"What size does he take?" Nan asked.

"I don't know. He just gave me this money and told me to buy a cap for him."

"Is he a big man?" Dorothy inquired, rummaging through the pile of caps again.

"No, he's sort of small, but his hair sticks up on top of his head."

"Well, this one's a medium," Dorothy said.

Almost instantly the boy tossed the money on the counter, grabbed the cap, and left.

"Did you hear that?" Nan said.

"What?" Dorothy replied absently.

"That man's description. It fits Albert Garry!"

Dorothy clapped her hand over her mouth. "Oh! You're right! Let's follow him!"

8

Chasing the Culprit

After a quick explanation to the Wellers, Nan and Dorothy left the booth.

"Where did he go?" Dorothy asked, looking through the crowd of visitors for the scrawny boy.

"This way," Nan said.

She hurried past a pizza stand toward a gazebo that stood at the center of the park. The area was filled with children carrying balloons and ice-cream cones. They seemed to be watching something, though Nan could not immediately see what it was. Her eyes were on the boy who had bought the cloth cap.

But as she and Dorothy approached him, he slipped away and vanished in the crowd of onlookers. The girls ran forward. "I don't see him anywhere," Dorothy said after a moment. "Do you, Nan?"

"No," she replied, weaving among the children with the balloons and ice cream.

The soft creamy swirls glinted in the sun, making the girl detectives hungry all of a sudden. But neither of them said a word. They worked their way to the front of the crowd, where a clown with big yellow curls was performing magic tricks. On the ground next to him was a basket with a cloth cap on top.

Momentarily confused, Nan looked at Dorothy, who shrugged. The clown did not resemble the one who had told them to go to the yellow tent, and he was too tall to be Albert Garry.

"We ought to talk to him anyway," Nan said, waiting for him to finish the performance. "For one thing, I'd like to find out if he knows Mr. Clown."

Finally, as the audience applauded, the two girls stepped toward the magician and introduced themselves. Nan asked if he knew the fuzzy red-haired clown.

"Not really," the man said. "He's new here."

"What's his name?" Dorothy inquired.

"Sorry. I don't know. You'd have to ask someone in Personnel. That's who hires everybody."

Nan revealed what had happened when the children went to the yellow tent. "Part of the bridge fell down," she said, "so we had to walk across the pond."

"That's a real shame," the clown said. "The park should've replaced that bridge a long time ago. It's always been a little rickety."

Dorothy glanced at the cap in the basket. "We were helping out at a booth here and sold a cap like this one just a few minutes ago," she remarked.

"Oh?" The clown shrugged. "It keeps the sun out of my eyes when I don't have this wig on."

As he strolled away, Dorothy spotted her young customer standing by a drinking fountain. He was holding the cap. "There he is!" she said, running up to him. "Didn't the cap fit?"

"Huh?" the boy responded with a puzzled look.

"The cap. Didn't it fit?" Nan repeated.

"I don't know. The man left before I could give it to him."

"That's too bad," she said sympathetically. "But there's always a chance he'll come back. If he does, will you tell us?"

Perplexed, the boy squinted at the girls. "Why?"

"We're working on a very important case," Dorothy blurted out.

"She means—well, you see—we think this man may be able to help us."

Before the boy could ask anything else, Nan and Dorothy left. "If it was Garry, we've missed him again," the Bobbsey girl said. "How about going to the Personnel Office? I'd like to find out more about Mr. Clown."

Dorothy agreed. They headed for the information building, where several men and women wearing name tags stood behind a long counter. Nan went up to a pleasant-faced woman in a lavender dress.

"Where is the Personnel Office?" Nan asked.

The woman blinked. "Are you girls looking for jobs?"

"No, we're too young for that," Dorothy said, smiling.

Nan explained the girls' purpose, and in a little while she and her cousin were led down a hallway to an office at the rear. Inside, they found a large table with a bin full of job application forms, and behind the table, two desks. One of them was empty.

The other one, however, was occupied by a hawk-nosed woman with large round gold-rimmed eyeglasses. "Yes?" she said without looking up.

Nan told about the collapse of the little footbridge, which Mrs. Weller had already reported, and how she and the other children had almost been stranded.

The woman pinched her lips together. "You weren't hurt, were you?" she asked.

"Oh, no," Nan answered.

"Good."

"We just want to find out a couple of things," Nan remarked. She mentioned the odd behavior of the clown with the fuzzy red hair and how she thought there might be a connection between him and the thief they were looking for.

"Just a minute," the woman said. She got up from her desk and went to a tall file that stood next to the side wall. She opened one of the drawers and sifted through a folder. "We have seventeen clowns on the premises. I don't know which one you are referring to."

Nan looked downhearted.

"I can't tell you any more than that. I'm sorry. These files are confidential."

Meanwhile, Bert, Harry, and the small twins had made their way to the Enchanted Castle.

Flossie skipped alongside Bert. "Maybe, if we took the princess some candy, she'd let us catch her," the little girl said with a mischievous grin.

"Look, Bert!" Freddie called. "There are some candy apples!" He pointed to a stand where a man was selling bright-red apples mounted on sticks.

"I'll buy them for you," Harry offered, pulling out his wallet.

Freddie and Flossie picked up two of the sticks.

"Ooey-gooey!" Flossie said, admiring the thick coat of hardened syrup.

"Let's have a duel!" Freddie cried suddenly. He held out the stick with the apple on it and lunged toward his twin. As he did so, the stick broke and the apple landed with a *plop* on Flossie's toe.

"Ouch!" she cried. "That hurt!"

Freddie apologized. "And I lost *my* apple, too!"

"If you'll promise to eat it, and not duel with it, I'll get you another one," Bert said.

"I promise," the boy replied.

When the children finished the apples, they hurried toward the castle. Flossie pointed out the sign to Harry. "We saw the princess the last time we were here," she said. "We tried to catch her, but she went behind a curtain and disappeared."

"Well, she won't get away this time," Harry bragged. "Bert and I will get her."

As before, when the children pushed open the little front door, a bell tinkled gently.

"The princess is in here!" Flossie whispered, tiptoeing toward the wide door that led from the entrance hall.

The children went in but stopped abruptly.

The brown curtain hung in front of the fireplace.

"Something's behind there!" Freddie declared. He ran across the room and jerked the curtain aside.

"I see her!" Flossie exclaimed as they watched two tiny silver slippers disappear up the chimney.

A soft, gentle voice drifted back to them. "Catch me if you can."

Wasting no more time, Bert dashed to the fireplace. He bent over and stared up the chimney.

"That's strange," he muttered. "Steps go up inside. There weren't any the other time. I remember looking for them!"

"Hurry, Bert!" Freddie exclaimed impatiently. "Let's go up!"

The stairs were narrow and very steep. Bert took the lead, followed by the younger twins and Harry.

"Ooh! It's spooky!" Flossie said, pulling herself up after her brother.

"I think we're coming to the end," Bert called to the others. The next minute he pushed open a door and stepped out onto a small balcony.

"Where's the princess? She's not here!" Flossie exclaimed, standing next to him.

"Here are some more stairs," Freddie announced. He had been walking around the balcony and had seen steps which led to the ground in back of the castle.

Quickly the four children ran down the stairs and around the little castle. But again there was no sign of the princess.

"Maybe the chimney stairs go up farther than we thought," Bert finally suggested. "She may be on the roof."

Freddie led the group this time. They climbed back up to the balcony but soon discovered there were no more steps.

"The princess must have gone out onto the balcony," Freddie insisted.

"But where is she now?" Flossie wailed, stepping outside.

As she spoke, the children heard something snap behind them. Turning to look, Bert and Harry groaned.

"The steps are gone!" Harry gasped.

All the children peered down the long, empty shaft through which they had climbed. Bert ran his hand along the inside wall, feeling the outline of one of the steps. He tugged on it as hard as he could, but nothing happened. The steps were locked in an upright position and would not move!

■ 9 ■
Island Hideout

"What'll we do?" Freddie asked bleakly.

"Stand back," Bert ordered. He gave one more yank on the top step, but again nothing happened. "Something must have tripped it off."

"Something or someone," Harry replied. He looked over the edge of the balcony and saw a man's head duck out of sight. "Is that Mr. Clown?"

"It could be," Flossie said, "'cept Mr. Clown had fuzzy red hair."

"He also wore a suit with big colored circles on it, right?" Bert said.

Flossie nodded as she and Freddie gazed at the fleeing figure. He was wearing a brown wig and a shiny white outfit with a little black vest and ruffled collar that made him look like a penguin.

"He probably changed his disguise," Harry

commented, "if he tore the last one in the woods."

"Well, I don't think he changed his height," Bert said. "This guy's a little shorter than Mr. Clown."

"Maybe it's Garry!" Freddie exclaimed suddenly.

Bert nodded as he watched the clown disappear into a building that housed the restaurant and gift shop. Then he turned to gaze at the opening that connected the balcony with the ground level and noticed an electronic lever at the base of the outside landing. He dived toward it instantly and pressed hard, unlocking the staircase. It swung back slowly and clicked into place again.

"Hooray!" the small twins shouted, scooting down the steps with their brother and Harry.

"You keep looking for the princess if you want to," Bert announced. "But I'm going after that clown! I'll meet you in front of the castle."

Harry agreed to stay with Freddie and Flossie while his cousin hurried outside.

"I think the princess is one of Santa's helpers," Flossie told her playmates.

"Why?" Freddie inquired.

"Because she went up the chimney!"

To their surprise, when they reached the entrance hall, there stood the phantom princess!

Sunlight poured over her through a small overhead window. She was a very small woman with wavy blond hair, clear blue eyes, and a smile that sparkled as much as her ballet costume and the wand she carried.

"Come here," she said, beckoning to the twins. "Tell me what you wish for the most."

"I wish . . ." Freddie said, pausing. "I wish for a big new fire engine!"

"And I need a new doll," Flossie replied. "May I have a new doll?"

The princess smiled. "I'm sure your wishes will be granted if you are good children. And now," she continued, "you are members of my Enchanted Castle. Here are your rewards!"

Going to a table in the hall, she returned with two little packages. "You may open them," she said.

Eagerly Freddie and Flossie untied the gold cord. In Flossie's box was a wand with a tinsel star at the top. In Freddie's was a tiny silver horn.

"Thank you!" the children exclaimed while Harry revealed what had happened to them upstairs.

"Someone must have triggered the steps off from below," he said.

"Well, *I* certainly wouldn't do such a thing," the young woman said, defending herself.

"Did you see anyone?" Harry went on. "A clown in a penguin suit?"

"A clown?" the princess repeated, wrinkling her forehead. "No, no clown. No one."

Thanking her again, the three children said good-bye and left. Outside again, they saw Bert coming across the pavement.

"Did you find him?" Harry called.

The other boy shook his head sullenly. "Too late, I guess. I went through the restaurant and the gift shop but he was already gone. He probably used one of the back doors."

Freddie and Flossie, meanwhile, displayed their new treasures.

"I asked the princess if she saw anyone enter the castle while we were there," Harry told his cousin, shifting his gaze to the younger twins.

"She didn't see anybody, Bert," Freddie answered.

When they returned to Mrs. Weller's booth, they told Nan and Dorothy about their most recent adventure. The girls, in turn, mentioned their own suspicion that Garry was in the park.

"We think he sent some kid over here to buy a cap to replace the one he lost when he stole Keith's canoe," Nan said.

"Did you tell all of this to the police?" Bert asked.

"Not yet," Nan replied. "We ended up talking

to one of the clowns and went to the information building to see what else we could find out."

When she finished speaking, Bert suggested they look for Officer Weaver. They found him at the entrance to the Underground City. Upon hearing the girls' story, he pushed his hat back and mopped his forehead.

"I don't see how Garry could still be in this park," he said. "We've been watching this place so carefully during the past week."

"We're positive he's either pretending to be a clown or he's working with one," Bert insisted.

"Impossible. We've already checked the ID of every employee. There isn't one person who matches Garry's description, and there isn't an extra clown in the park."

"Oh," Bert said, giving a solemn nod.

"Thanks anyhow, kids."

After he left, Nan complimented her brother. "I still think it's a possibility—Garry dressing up as a clown."

"So do I," Bert replied. "Garry could have stolen the clown costumes. If he's hiding out in the park, he can change costumes whenever he wants to and sneak around without ever being caught."

"Then why would he ask that kid to buy him a cap?" Harry inquired.

"It's just another way of disguising himself,"

Nan said, "at least, when he thinks we're not around. When he asked for the cap, Garry must've been planning his escape. But he saw you go into the castle and wanted to make sure you didn't interfere."

"So he put on that penguin suit and followed us. When he was sure no one could see him, he locked the stairway," Bert concluded. "You know what?"

"What?"

"He couldn't be working alone."

Later, at the supper table, Bert asked Uncle William if a report had come in about the stolen boat.

The man shook his head gloomily.

"Maybe someone along the lakeshore has seen it," the boy suggested. "We'll ask, if you want."

"By all means. I wish you would."

After supper the older children went over to the lake. They walked along the shore road, stopping at each cottage to inquire about the missing motorboat. No one remembered having seen it since the evening of the Water Carnival.

"Bert, do you think we'll ever catch Garry?" Harry asked.

The boy detective looked blankly at his cousin. "Do I have to answer that?" he said.

The next morning Bert thought of his resolve

to explore the island where Freddie and Flossie had heard the threatening voice. Mentioning it to his mother again, he said, "It's the only chance we have to solve the mystery. Please, Mom."

Mrs. Bobbsey hesitated. "Oh, all right. I suppose you'll be okay all together. But don't stay too long."

Upon hearing the news, Dorothy suggested they call Keith. "Maybe he'll take us in his canoe," she said, prompting Bert to go to the telephone.

But Keith said his canoe could not hold all of them. "I'm sure I can get hold of that rowboat Freddie and Flossie borrowed the other day. I'll meet you at the boathouse at eleven."

When the Bobbseys and Dorothy arrived, Keith was waiting by the canoe and rowboat, which were drawn up on the bank side by side.

"We bought a dozen chocolate doughnuts!" Flossie said with a grin.

"Wow!" Keith said, eyeing the bag in her hand.

It was decided that Bert, Nan, and Flossie would go in Keith's canoe, while Dorothy and Harry would take Freddie in the other craft.

Soon the boats rounded the bend of the shoreline. The island lay just in front of them.

"This'll be fun even if we don't find anyone

on the island," Dorothy said as they touched shore. Bert jumped out and held Keith's canoe steady.

Nan, meanwhile, stepped ashore and turned to take the bag of doughnuts from Flossie. But the canoe tipped, causing her to teeter back and forth.

"Look out!" Keith shouted as the bag slid from Flossie's hand. Nan lunged forward instantly and caught it.

"Whew! Good catch!" Bert congratulated her.

Then Keith shook his head in mock despair. "And I thought my doughnuts were going to the fishes for sure!" he said impishly.

By this time Harry and Dorothy had beached their rowboat and helped Freddie carry a grocery bag full of sandwiches and soft drinks.

"Do you want to eat first or explore?" Nan asked.

"Let's eat!" Freddie spoke up. "I'm hungry!"

"This looks like a good place," Keith observed, indicating the clean white beach.

The island was thickly wooded, but on three sides it was bordered by fine powdery sand. Nan and Dorothy, with Flossie's help, spread out a cloth, then settled down to eat. Before they finished, however, Bert gave a yell and held up his arm. A giant crab was clinging to his wrist! The boy jerked his arm as hard as he could. The crab flew off and landed some distance away.

"Oh, Bert, did it nip you?" Nan asked anxiously as she ran to her brother.

Bert examined his wrist. "No, but it sure did pinch a lot!"

As Dorothy started to walk over to the crab, Harry shrieked, "Look out!"

Dorothy ignored him. She bent over and picked it up. "Don't worry. It won't hurt you," she said, tossing it to Bert.

He jumped aside and stared down sheepishly. "It's rubber!" he exclaimed. "I guess we're even now."

"No more setting off alarm clocks." Dorothy giggled.

"Okay."

Still laughing over the incident, the children gathered up the remains of the picnic. Then Bert surveyed the landscape behind them.

"I want to find out who scared Freddie and Flossie the other day," he said.

Keith excused himself to make sure the boats were safe. He pulled them farther up on the beach. "I'd hate to be marooned here!" he said.

"Does anyone live on this island, Dot?" Nan asked as the group went into the woods.

"I don't think so. At least, I don't know of anybody."

The woods seemed very quiet. Even the birds

were still. Then a honking sound broke the silence.

"What's that?" Flossie asked in surprise.

"Tree frogs," Dorothy said. She put her finger to her lips and tiptoed over to a little bush. "There."

Clinging to a branch were two grayish-brown frogs not more than two inches long. Their throats were puffed out into round yellow sacs.

"They're blowing up!" Flossie whispered.

"They do that when they're talking to each other," Dorothy explained.

"Come on, Freddie and Flossie," Bert called. "Stay with us so you don't get lost."

The children went on deeper into the woods until they came to a little brook, and took off their sneakers to wade across. On the other side Bert observed a small, crude-looking shelter. Several branches had been placed across the space between two trees, the ends resting in the notches where the limbs met the tree trunk. Leafy branches had been laid over these to form a roof.

"Someone had a campfire here," Nan declared, stooping to feel the bits of burnt wood and ash. "It's still warm!"

"Which means that whoever built this hasn't been gone long!" Bert said. "If it was Garry, he might still be nearby!"

■ 10 ■
Motorboat Mischief

"I wonder where he could be," Harry said, looking downstream.

"We'll have to fan out and search," Bert suggested. "Nan, you and Keith take the left. Harry and Dorothy, the right. I'll go straight ahead with Freddie and Flossie. If you see anyone, give a shout and the rest of us will come!"

They followed Bert's instructions, and once more the search went forward. But they had no success. Half an hour later the three groups met back on the beach.

"It's no use," Bert said in a discouraged tone. "He must have left before we arrived."

As Bert spoke, Dorothy gazed at the sky with its puffy black clouds. "We'd better go home," she said worriedly. "A storm is coming, and this lake can get pretty rough."

The children put the grocery bag in Keith's canoe quickly and took their places. But as

Harry shoved off in the rowboat, a brilliant streak of lightning flashed across the sky. Nan, who was seated in the canoe, noticed someone near the beach.

"There's a man in a motorboat!" she called. "Is it the *Firefly*, Dot?"

"Motorboat? Where?" the other girl said.

"Just leaving that far stretch of beach. I didn't see a boat there before. He must have hidden it under the trees."

Dorothy studied the boat intently. "It could be ours," she said. "I'm not sure."

"I wish we could catch up to it," Keith put in, "but we can't in the canoe."

The children watched as the motorboat sped toward the other side of the island and disappeared.

"I'd better tell the police," Dorothy said. "I'll race you to shore!" She dug her oars into the water and sent the rowboat leaping forward.

Bert and Keith paddled after her furiously.

The wind, however, had begun to gust, making the lake water choppy. It took all the children's strength to push through the waves as water crashed against the boats.

"I hope we get home before it starts to pour!" Dorothy said, feeling a light sprinkle against her cheeks. "It's shallow here, but you ought to see how rough it gets in a high wind!"

The trip home seemed to take forever. But at last the voyagers ran their craft up to the boathouse.

"I'll put everything away," Keith offered.

Bert and Harry stayed to help, however, while Nan, Dorothy, and the small twins hurried to the Minturn house. Just as they reached the porch, a burst of rain came down in torrents.

Mrs. Bobbsey opened the door. "I'm so glad you're home," she said. "I was worried you'd get caught in the storm!"

Nan told her mother that Bert and Harry would be along as soon as the boats were locked in the boathouse. She mentioned having seen a motorboat that looked like the Minturns'.

"I'll call the police right away," Aunt Emily said.

Freddie, in the meantime, had gone off to find Snoop. In a while he reported to the others that the cat had disappeared.

"I can't find him anywhere!" he declared. "I hope he's not outside. Snoop's afraid of storms."

The children put on slickers, rainhats, and boots and ran out to look. They searched under all the bushes without finding the missing cat. Then Freddie went into the garage.

"Here, Snoop," he called, brushing raindrops off his nose.

A faint meow answered back. Stooping down,

Freddie gazed under Uncle William's car. There, rolled up in a little black ball, was Snoop!

"Come on out, Snoop," the boy coaxed. But the cat refused to budge. "All right, I'll get you," the boy said, wriggling under the vehicle. He reached out, grasped the animal, and inched his way back.

"You found him!" Flossie said happily as her brother carried his pet up to the porch.

"Why don't you put him in the house," Nan suggested, "and watch the storm with us?"

By this time the ocean was a mass of white-caps.

"Look at the waves!" Flossie said, focusing on the flooded shoreline. "They're so big!"

Just then she saw Keith charging toward the house. He was wearing an old blue raincoat that he had found hanging in the boathouse.

"Someone's in trouble on the lake!" he shouted.

"We'd better call the police," Dorothy said, starting for the door. "They have a rescue launch."

The officer in charge assured the girl that help would be sent immediately.

"Let's go up to the police boathouse," she suggested, putting down the receiver. "It's not far from here."

When Nan went in the house to tell her mother where they were going, Mrs. Bobbsey insisted that the younger twins stay at home. "I don't want you to blow away," she said.

"See you later," the other children said, running down to the lakeshore.

"I don't see the boat," Harry observed as they reached the water.

"There it is!" Keith pointed out across the gray lake.

Straining their eyes, the children could barely see the small craft tossing up and down on the stormy water. It was out of control.

"It's probably flooded!" Dorothy cried out fearfully.

She led the way along the shore until they came to the headquarters of the police lake patrol. As the group approached, two officers had begun boarding a trim launch.

"We're going right out!" one of the men said, recognizing Dorothy.

"May we go with you?" Bert asked.

"It's pretty dangerous out there. I don't think so."

"We won't get in the way. We might even be able to help," Keith spoke up.

The officer looked at the tall boy. "Well, we are shorthanded," he said. "Maybe you can help us. It's rough out there, though. If you want to, you can stay in the wheelhouse with the pilot, Bill Cooper."

Everyone nodded.

"By the way, my name is Fred Palmer."

Bill Cooper took his place at the wheel of the launch while Fred Palmer walked to the stern, where there was a post with a rope around it.

Dorothy climbed aboard the boat and followed the policeman into the wheelhouse. She sat down on the narrow bench under the window.

Nan came next. As she stepped on the wet deck, her feet slipped out from under her and she skidded across the wood planks, straight for the opening in the railing!

Bert dived after her and grabbed the back of Nan's raincoat.

"Whew! It's a good thing you caught me!" Nan exclaimed as she scrambled to her feet. "Thanks!"

Shakily she made her way forward to join Dorothy, while the boys clung to the rail near the stern. Now the launch sped on through the foamy white water.

Heavy sheets of rain obscured the stricken boat in the distance.

"He can't keep it afloat much longer," Cooper said grimly.

As the police launch drew nearer, however, Dorothy stood up and looked through the window. "That's our boat!" she exclaimed in astonishment.

In another minute the patrolman cut the motor. Palmer picked up a bullhorn and called to the man in the drifting boat, "Are you all right?"

The occupant, who had huddled in the bottom, sat up slowly. He cupped his hands and shouted back, "Yes. But the motor has conked out!"

The pilot of the launch pulled as close to the motorboat as he could without upsetting it. "I'll throw you a tow!" Palmer said.

He unwound the rope from the post and tossed it toward the stranded boat. *Plop!* It fell into the water, just missing the craft as it drifted away. Palmer hauled in the rope and tried again. This time the other man grabbed it and tied it around one of the seats. Suddenly a high wave struck, tilting the boat at a precarious angle, and the man teetered.

"I can't swim!" he cried out, trying to regain his balance. Then another wave slapped against the craft, sending him over the side!

Without a word, Bert stripped off his slicker and boots and dived into the lake. Officer Palmer soared after him. But by the time he hit the

water, the boy detective had already reached the victim. The patrolman swam toward them and, between him and Bert, they carried the man to the launch. Harry and Keith leaned over and pulled him up. The rescuers, meantime, tied the disabled motorboat to the stern of the launch, then climbed on board. The stranger sank to the deck, coughing and shivering.

Nan and Dorothy ran out of the wheelhouse with blankets, which they put around the three swimmers.

"Cooper has a thermos of hot tea," Palmer said to Keith. "Get it, will you?"

"Sure," the boys said, disappearing to get cups for everyone.

The stranger sat up and sipped the steaming liquid. He was thin and blond and, though his hair was drenched, one lock stood up limply on the crown of his head.

Bert stared at him. "Aren't you Albert Garry?" he asked.

On hearing Bert's question, the stranger appeared startled. Then he closed his eyes and weakly shook his head no.

"I guess he's all in," Officer Palmer remarked. "We'll take him into the wheelhouse."

When the shivering man was finally seated for the ride back, the policeman returned to the children, who were still on deck. The rain had stopped almost entirely.

"Do you know this man?" the officer asked Bert.

"I think he's a thief," the boy detective replied.

He told Palmer how he and the other children had tried to capture the man who had stolen money from an airline.

The patrolman whistled in surprise. "If you're right," he said, "if this boat thief is Albert Garry, a lot of people will be very grateful to you."

"Even if he isn't Garry," Dorothy put in, "he had our boat!"

"We'll take him to headquarters for questioning," Palmer said.

Soon the police launch pulled alongside the dock. Palmer grabbed a line to throw over the mooring post. As the rope coiled around the anchor, however, the suspect bolted from the wheelhouse. "Catch him!" Cooper shouted. But the man had already vaulted over the railing onto the dock.

Bert and Keith ran after him. Palmer stopped only long enough to make the line fast, then joined in the chase.

When the fugitive reached the end of the dock, he hesitated a moment, as if trying to decide which way to run. Bert made a flying tackle and grabbed the man's feet. With a crash, the stranger fell to the ground.

"Good work!" Palmer shouted, pounding after them. He jerked the man to his feet and snapped handcuffs on him.

"You have a lot of explaining to do," he said to the prisoner. Thanking the children for their help, he herded the man toward a waiting patrol car.

"He has to be Albert Garry!" Nan declared with excitement.

"It sure looks that way!" Harry chimed in.

"At least we've got our boat back," Dorothy reminded everybody. "Maybe it just needs gas."

As the boys carried over a can, Keith's eyes traveled to one of the seats. Under it was a soggy brown wig along with some clothing. Bert leapt to retrieve it.

"What's this?" he said, holding up a soiled white costume with a black vest. "Wait a minute. This is what the clown who tried to lock us in the castle was wearing!"

When the boys showed Nan and Dorothy what they had found, Nan's face beamed. "I knew it!" she said.

"But we don't know that the man we rescued *is* Garry," Dorothy said.

"Even if he isn't, he has to be connected somehow. Why would he bother to make trouble for us otherwise? He had to know we were looking for the airline thief."

"Nan's right," Bert said. He wrung the clothes to squeeze out any excess water and carried them to the Minturns' house. "I'll call headquarters and tell them what we found."

Officer Weaver answered. After listening to Bert's discovery, he said, "Hang on to the clothes. We'll want them for evidence. That man you caught refuses to say anything. An official from Allied Cargo Airlines is on his way over to identify him. I'll let you know what happens."

The children stayed close to the house all afternoon, but it was almost suppertime before the phone rang. Bert dashed to answer it.

"Congratulations, you caught Albert Garry, all right!" Weaver said. "That airline official made a positive identification."

"Terrific," Bert replied.

"There's one problem, though. He won't tell us where the money is!"

■ 11 ■
A Lot of Loot

When Bert told the news to the others, Flossie smiled. "Bert caught the bad man!" she said proudly.

"Now, if we could just find the money," Nan remarked.

"Maybe he hid it on the island."

"I suppose we could go back there and look around again," Dorothy said.

Flossie wrinkled her nose. "When Cindy saw the man, he had a shopping bag."

"With the money in it!" Freddie exclaimed.

"We don't know that for certain," Nan objected. "He could have hidden the loot anywhere."

Bert, who had remained silent throughout the discussion, spoke up. "Well, I vote we go back to the amusement park and look for the bag. Even if it doesn't contain the stolen money, it may hold other clues."

The others agreed. When Nan revealed the plan to her mother, Mrs. Bobbsey sighed but gave her permission. "I know you won't be happy until you've solved the mystery completely."

"Thanks, Mom," Nan said, hugging her mother.

Later, at the park, they went immediately to the Weller booth first. They told Cindy and her mother about the capture of Albert Garry.

"I still think he hid the money in the Underground City," Freddie stated. "I know I saw him in there."

Bert reminded his little brother that the police had searched the Underground City thoroughly but had found absolutely nothing.

"Then maybe the money is hidden outside the City," Flossie observed.

"Good idea!" Bert said. "Let's go see."

Cindy was as excited as the other children. "May I help them look, Mother?" she asked Mrs. Weller.

"Of course you may."

When the group reached the entrance, the ride was doing a brisk business. Little boats were leaving the dock every few minutes.

The low green wooden structure that housed the City was surrounded by shrubbery.

"Let's separate," Nan said. She, Dorothy,

Harry, and Flossie went around one side of the building while Bert, Freddie, Cindy, and Keith went around the other. They looked under all the bushes, and when they met in front again, no one had found the elusive shopping bag.

Suddenly Cindy had another thought. "There's a small hollow in back of the City," she said. "Maybe the thief went down there."

"What are we waiting for!" Bert cried, darting ahead of the others. As Cindy described it, the land dropped off sharply into a ravine overgrown with bushes.

Freddie and Flossie were the first to scramble down the incline, followed by the others. A few minutes passed while everyone pushed aside the thick shrubbery. Then Flossie gave a squeal. "Here's something!" she said, pulling out a white paper bag. It was covered with blue stars!

While the other children watched breathlessly, Bert put his hand in the bag and drew out a pack of currency.

"There must be a fortune here!" Harry cried as his cousin opened the bag wide for everyone to see inside.

"We'd better call the police!" Nan exclaimed.

Hurriedly Bert stuffed the money back into the bag, and the children made their way up to the entrance of the Underground City. From there they ran to Mrs. Weller's booth, where Bert told of their exciting discovery.

"May we leave the money here while I call the police?" the boy asked.

"We'll guard it," Freddie volunteered, drawing a smile from the woman as the older twins left.

It was not long before a patrol car appeared in front of Mrs. Weller's booth. Passersby gaped as Officer Weaver jumped out and raced to the counter, where Freddie proudly handed over the shopping bag.

"I'd like all of you"—the policeman looked at Cindy also—"to come down to headquarters with me," he said, tossing the money to the other officer in the back of the car. "Bert, you and Nan ride up front with me. The others can squeeze in the back with Officer Palmer."

Their friend from the lake patrol smiled warmly. "I see you're following right through on this case!" he teased. "We'll have to make you honorary members of the force pretty soon!"

"We're already detectives!" Flossie said.

In a short while the patrol car drew up to Ocean Cliff police headquarters. "Maybe our friend Garry will talk when he sees this bag of groceries!" Officer Weaver said with a grin, putting the money on the chief's desk.

After he had met all the children, the chief

ordered Albert Garry to be brought in. The prisoner glared at the children as he shuffled into the room. When he saw the white shopping bag, however, he turned pale.

"Does this look familiar to you, Mr. Garry?" the chief asked sternly. "These children found it in Lakeside Amusement Park, and they tell me you were seen carrying it the day the money was stolen from the airline."

The man clenched his teeth and took a deep breath but said nothing.

"You might as well tell us. Things will go easier for you if you do."

Again, there was silence.

"I saw you!" Cindy exclaimed, causing the man's face to redden again.

"So what?" he growled. "So I took the money while we were unloading the plane. When the cops got on my trail and followed me to Lakeside, I hid it."

"I saw you in the Underground City!" Freddie piped up.

"I would have gotten away if that mob of cops hadn't swarmed over the park. I suppose you kids started that!"

"No," the police chief corrected. "But the Bobbseys and their friends have been a great help to us."

"Pretending to be one of the clowns was clever

of you," Nan said, explaining her theory to the police.

"But not clever enough," Bert added. "You thought you could scare us. Putting that red wig in the tree was just a ruse to make sure we crossed the footbridge."

"So you could knock it down," Dorothy concluded.

"That bridge was already broken," Garry shot back.

"How did you know that?" asked Nan.

"My cousin told me."

"He's one of the clowns, isn't he?" Bert said. "He overheard us talking about you and told you to be on the lookout for us. He even sent us on that wild-goose chase to the tent and loaned you his wig."

"Then you probably got the idea of wearing his costumes, too," Nan put in, "especially when you wanted to play a trick on us."

"When you tried trapping me in the castle, for instance," Bert said.

"Look, every time I thought I had my escape route figured out, you kids popped up. I had to keep you occupied," the thief said, sneering. "Besides, I liked being a clown. I got around the park free as a bird. No questions asked."

"How *did* you manage to get away from us?" Officer Weaver questioned. "You might as well tell us. Where were you hiding before we picked you up yesterday?"

The captive admitted that he had stolen Keith's canoe from the lagoon while the boys were onshore registering for the Water Carnival. "The cops were watching all the exits, but it didn't occur to them I could leave by water!" he said.

"Go on!" the police chief directed.

"Well, I beached the canoe, thinking I could get a bus or something and come back later for the money," he said, "you know, after all the excitement had died down."

"But you didn't do that," Nan spoke up. "You stayed around Ocean Cliff. Why?"

"Because I suddenly realized that I could hide out on the island. I took a motorboat—"

"Ours," Dorothy interrupted.

"Without it I figured your papa couldn't follow me. Anyhow, I set up a little camp for myself."

"You're the one who told Freddie and me to leave, aren't you?" Flossie said accusingly. She turned to the police chief. "That was the day we lost our toy sailboat."

"I see," the chief said.

Garry looked disgusted as he spoke. "These kids were always in the way." He looked at Nan and Dorothy with cold, steely eyes. "The next day when I went back to the park to get the money, I saw these two girls follow the boy I sent to buy me a cap."

"So that's why you took off so fast," Dorothy commented. "He wondered what had happened to you. Now we know."

"After the castle bit, I decided to sit it out on the island, and then the next thing I knew, this whole bunch decided to have a picnic there!" Garry shook his head in despair. "I got away in the boat, but then the motor went."

Dorothy sizzled but kept quiet.

"I want you to know it was these same children who reported your trouble on the lake. If they hadn't done that, you would have drowned," Officer Weaver said.

"I know," Garry said grudgingly.

The chief motioned to have the prisoner returned to his cell, after which he said to the children, "The Ocean Cliff police have a lot to thank you for."

He stood to shake hands with the Bobbseys as well as the other children. "Without your sharp eyes and quick thinking, we might never have captured this man. We'll pick up his cousin, too. I want you to meet Mr. Evans, president of Allied Cargo Airlines, and tell him how you solved this case."

The children were eager to tell their parents

about the exciting events of the afternoon. That night at the supper table the full story of Garry and the hidden money unfolded.

Mr. Bobbsey said, "I'm glad you solved all your mysteries, because the summer is almost over and we have to go home to Lakeport."

Did the end of summer mean there would be no more mysteries to solve? the young detectives wondered. They would be happy to discover the exciting *Mystery at School* as soon as they returned!

"We can't go until we tell Mr. Evans all about Mr. Garry and the money!" Flossie spoke up.

Freddie took up the plea. "Flossie's right. The police chief told us to tell Mr. Evans."

Mr. Bobbsey laughed. "Well, I can see you have a few more things to do here. I, unfortunately, have to get home!"

"Richard," said Mrs. Bobbsey, "why don't you go back to Lakeport tomorrow? The twins and I will leave here in a few days."

"That's the best thing to do," her husband said. "What about Harry?"

Mrs. Bobbsey addressed the boy. "Your parents called while you were out and want you on the train for Meadowbrook tomorrow."

"Oh, everybody's leaving!" Dorothy sighed.

"We're not," Flossie said, gazing up at her cousin.

"Yes, you are."

"Not right away," added Freddie.

After their father and Harry had left the next day, the children busied themselves swimming in the ocean and taking boat rides on the lake. Then two days later, the doorbell rang after breakfast. Aunt Emily went to answer it.

A stocky white-haired man introduced himself as Mr. Evans.

"Nan? Bert?" she called. "Freddie? Flossie?"

The children hurried into the living room with Dorothy.

"I was told I would probably find all of you here," he said.

Freddie and Flossie smiled.

"I want to thank you, on behalf of Allied Cargo Airlines, for finding that thief Albert Garry and the money he stole from the plane shipment. I understand you had quite an adventure."

"Oh, we did!" Flossie said. "We almost got trapped in the Enchanted Castle!"

"You did? How?"

She explained about Garry's clown disguise.

"That wasn't all," Bert noted. "Before that happened, someone else told us to meet him at a yellow tent."

Seeing the puzzlement in Mr. Evans's face, Nan explained how the man and his cousin were connected.

"Anyway, after we got there, there was no one around," Nan continued. "Then the little bridge fell down and we had to wade across the lake to get back."

"That's awful," Mr. Evans remarked. "Did anything else happen?"

"Oh, lots of things," Dorothy said, describing how Garry had stolen her family's motorboat and gotten caught in the storm. "He fell overboard, but Bert saved him."

The boy blushed. "Officer Palmer and I both saved him," he said.

"We had fun solving all the mysteries at the seashore," Freddie put in.

"Well, I'm glad to hear it," the company president said, "and to show my appreciation, I'd like to give you a reward. Any ideas?"

There was silence for several seconds. Then Freddie spoke. "I'd like a ride in a helicopter!"

"We all would!" Nan said.

The next morning Mrs. Minturn received a secret telephone call. She asked Dorothy and the Bobbseys to go for a drive with her. After a while she turned into the entrance to the airport.

"Are we really going to ride in a helicopter?" Freddie asked.

"That's only part of the surprise," Aunt Emily said mysteriously.

She parked the car and led the way onto the airfield, where a jumbo helicopter was waiting, along with the pilot, Cindy, and Keith.

"Cindy! Keith!" Nan exclaimed.

"We're going, too!" Cindy said. "The police chief told Mr. Evans we were part of your detective team."

"You sure are!" the twins replied.

"All aboard for a whirlybird flight to a picnic on a deserted island!" the pilot said.

"Wowee!" Freddie cheered.

They all hurried up the steps, and soon the helicopter rose into the sky. A while later, the children could see a small wooded island below them.

"Our own deserted island!" Flossie said excitedly.

"I don't ever want to be rescued from here!" Freddie said.

"Not even by sending a message in a bottle?" Dorothy said, snickering.

All the others laughed, even Bert.